WELL HUNG

by

Tony Ellis

Published by Ideas Unlimited (Publishing)

Published by:
Ideas Unlimited (Publishing)
P.O. Box 125, Portsmouth
Hampshire PO1 4PP

ISBN 1 871964 07 5

Ideas first hung in 'Fiesta', Britains favourite top shelf magazine.

Printed and bound in Great Britain.

"BEEN HERE LONG?"

"OH, AND BY THE WAY, THE PLACE IS
HAUNTED."

"YOU HAVE A CHOICE OF COLOURS, LADS ..
.. 'SNOT GREEN', 'DIARRHOEA BROWN', OR
'RUNNING SORE YELLOW'."

"AND NOT ONLY THAT .... THE BLOODY
BELL DOESN'T WORK ANYWAY."

IN CASE OF
FIRE
PISS

"WE'RE NOT ALLOWED LAXATIVES, BUT IF YOU ASK HIM NICELY HE'LL BEAT THE SHIT OUT OF YOU."

"SADISTIC BASTARDS! WHEN THEY PROMISED US TV, I KNEW THERE WOULD BE A CATCH."

"WHAT DO YOU MEAN F . . . OFF . . . . . .?
I SAID I'VE WORKED OUT A PLAN."

"CHEESE ON TOAST AGAIN TONIGHT."

"YES, I SUPPOSE THEY ARE A BIT TOUGHER ON YOU SEX OFFENDERS."

"AND NO GETTING UP TO ANY FUNNY BUSINESS WITH THE NEW PRISONER!"

**"TOILET FACILITIES HERE ARE
ATROCIOUS."**

"ECONOMICAL AND MORE EFFECTIVE ....
IT BUGGERS UP OUR SENSE OF
COMRADESHIP TOO."

"IT'S THEIR WAY OF DISCOURAGING SEXY THOUGHTS!"

"THE SNOOKER TABLE'S BROKEN . . . WE'RE HAVING TO IMPROVISE."

"THE FLUSHING SYSTEM TAKES SOME GETTING USED TO . . . . WE DON'T GET TO CRAP UNTIL IT RAINS."

THEY'RE REQUESTING CONTINENTAL
FLAVOURED FOOD . . . . . GET THAT LITTLE
GREEK PLATE WASHER TO CRAP IN THE
SWILL."

"NOT LOOKING AT HER WILL ONLY DELAY
AN ERECTION, MATE . . . . IN A MOMENT
SHE'LL START TALKING DIRTY."

"IT'S TO DISCOURAGE GLUTTONY .... THE
PAIN IS BEARABLE IF YOU DON'T CRAP A
LOT."

"IT'S A SEXUAL AID . . . . IN HERE IT'S THE NEAREST YOU'LL GET TO A WANK."

"RIGHT! HANDS UP ALL THOSE WHO WANT A PUNCH ON THE NOSE . . . . OH! ALL OF YOU!"

"TEA TASTES LIKE GNAT'S PISS, DOES IT?
WELL, YOU'RE HALF RIGHT . . . . . IT'S
GUARDS PISS."

"INGENIOUS ISN'T IT? DESIGNED TO STOP US PISSING ON OUR FEET."

"IT STOPS THE DISPUTES OVER BULL-EYES. THEY GET AN AUDIBLE INDICATION WHEN SOMEONE HITS ONE."

"THIRTY SEVEN .... THIRTY EIGHT ...."

"HAVE YOU NOTICED? EVERY TIME WE BREATH IN, HIS THINGY RISES."

"IT'S THE ONLY SUPPORT I'M ALLOWED ....
UNDERWEAR EXCITES THE GUARDS."

"BLOODY HELL, MAN! . . . . CAN'T YOU
ASK'EM TO PUT SOMETHING IN YOUR
COCOA?"

"YOU STILL HAVE ONE LAST HOPE, SANDRA
.... TELL HIM YOU HAVE A HEADACHE!"

"WE DON'T LIKE TO SEE NEW GUYS ATTEMPT TO ESCAPE. IN FACT . . . . IT BRINGS TEARS TO OUR EYES."

"IT'S A NEW INVENTION TO SAVE ON
TOILET PAPER, LADS.... YOU SPIN DRY."

"IT'S AN EMOTIONAL TORTURE .... THEY SCREW UP OUR FAVOURITE TUNES."

"BASTARDS! ONE SEXY THOUGHT AND THE WHOLE DAMN PLACE KNOWS ABOUT IT."

"I DON'T MIND GIVING BLOOD, BUT THIS IS SODDIN' RIDICULOUS!"

"I SHOULDN'T MENTION YOUR PILES . . . IF MY APPENDICITIS OP IS ANYTHING TO GO BY."

" . . . . . . SAYS HE'S A FREEMASON . . . HE
COULD GET US OUT OF THIS SHIT IF ONLY
HE COULD GIVE SOMEONE A FANCY
HANDSHAKE!"

"RELAX, DAMMIT! I KNOW IT'S NOT MUCH
OF A SEX LIFE, BUT IT'S ALL WE'VE GOT."

"IT'S A NEW RECREATIONAL ACTIVITY FOR
THE SCREWS . . . . A SPONSORED
'STARVE'."

"YOUR TESTICLES ARE THE LEAST OF YOUR
WORRIES, SUNSHINE . . . . THEY ALWAYS
AIM FOR A DOUBLE TOP TO START."

"SO IT'S OVERCROWDED . . . . AT LEAST
NOW WE HAVE SOME SORT OF SEX LIFE."

"THEY SAY IT HAPPENS TO ALL OF THE
LONG-TERM LADS EVENTUALLY, DEAR . . . .
SORRY, JOE."

"IT'S DESIGNED TO TITILLATE YOU MEN . . . . ONE TOUCH AND I RIPPLE FOR HOURS."

"IT WAS A MISTAKE ASKING HER FOR A BLOW JOB."

"YOU NOW OWN A FORTNIGHTS'
ACCOMMODATION ON NINE FEET OF
ALCATRAZ WALL EACH JUNE .... HAVE A
NICE DAY!"

"RIGHT! YOU UNCOOPERATIVE LITTLE BASTARD! WE'VE DECIDED TO CONVERT YOU INTO A STILL-LIFE."

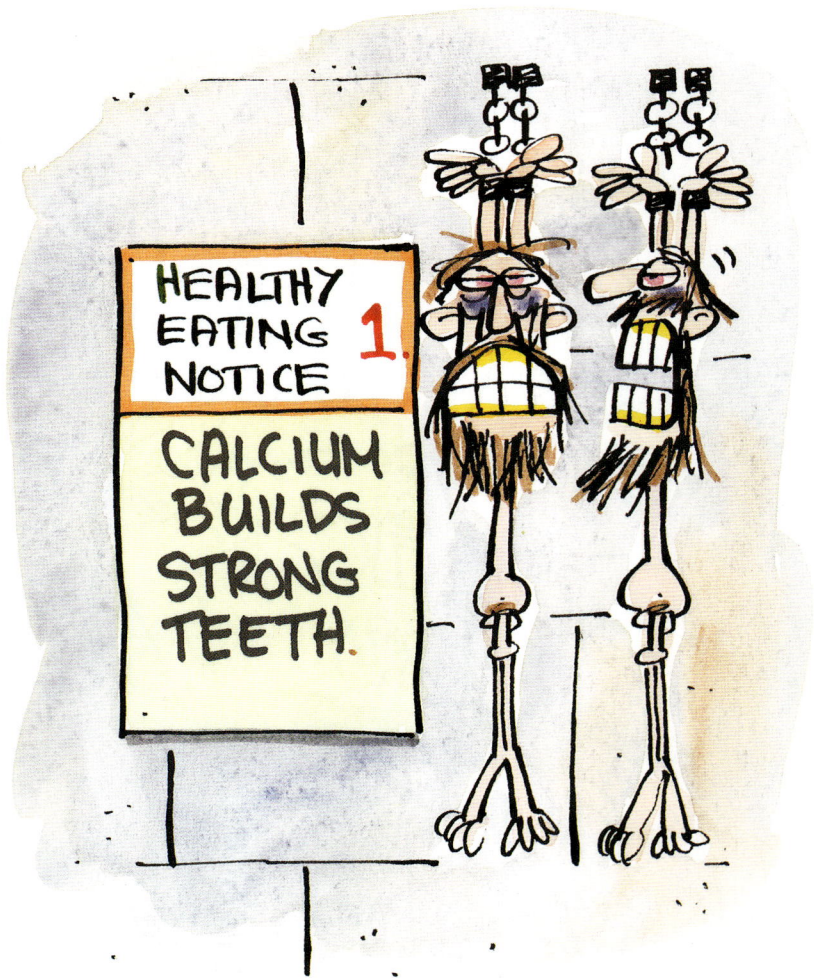

"WE GET ENOUGH SODDIN' CALCIUM! . . . . .
WHEN THE HELL ARE WE GOING TO GET
SOME PROTEIN?"

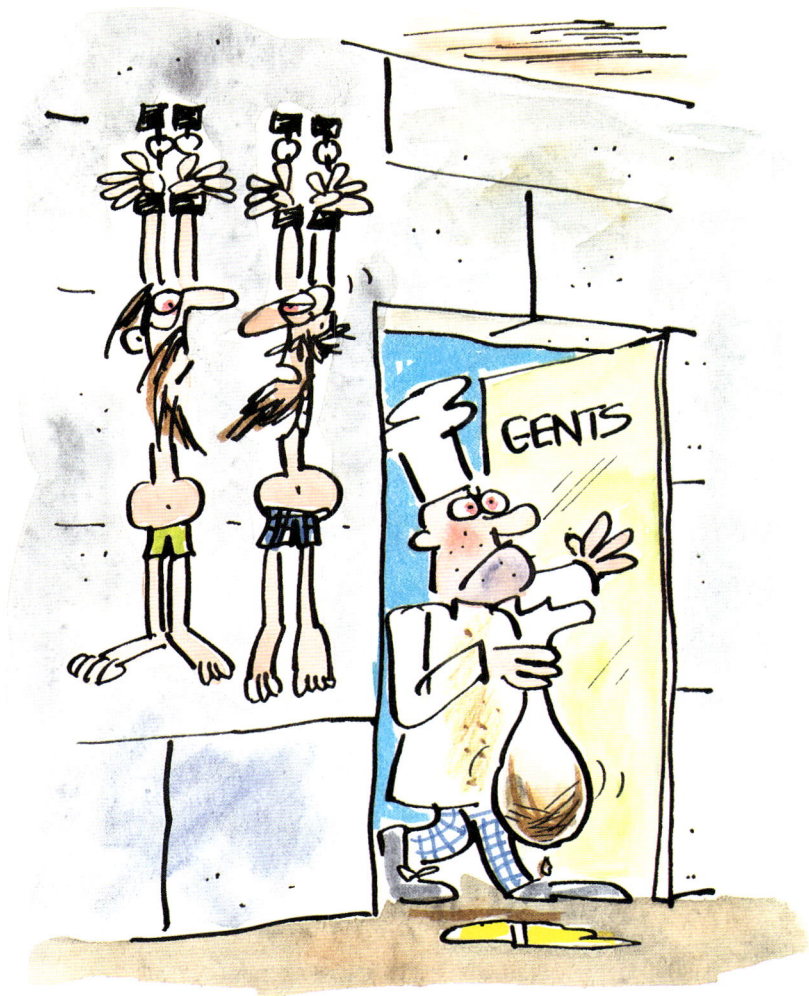

"I THINK WE'RE GOING TO REGRET ASKING HIM WHAT SORT OF CRAP HE HAS PLANNED FOR TODAYS MENU!"

"WELL, THAT'S IT THEN! NOW WE'LL NEVER STOP THE BUGGER FLICKING BOGIES IN THE PORRIDGE!"

"THAT'S THE IDEA, LADS, SHIT AWAY ....
AND ON A RAINY DAY YOU EVEN GET YOUR
ARSES WASHED."

"COURSE IT'S NOT UNHEALTHY . . . . YOU GET MORE FRESH AIR THAN YOUR MATES."

"WE COULD DO WITH A COUPLE OF SOPRANOS. LET'S CASTRATE THE MIDDLE TWO."

"HE'S CERTAINLY BUGGERED UP THE PLEASURES OF FAMILY VISITS."

"IT'S A VENEREAL DISEASE . . . . I CAUGHT
IT OFF MY WIFE."

"DON'T THINK MUCH OF THESE CHRISTMAS GET-TOGETHERS, DO YOU?"

"OH MY GOD! I THINK HE'S GOING TO TRY OUT HIS NEW NUT CRACKERS."

"THAT'S FUNNY! I DON'T REMEMBER PUTTING THE SAUCE ON THE CHRISTMAS PUDDING!"

"CHRISTMAS IS DEPRESSING ENOUGH, BUT BOXING DAY IS PURE BLOODY HELL!"

"THE PAIN EASES WHEN IT REACHES THE FLOOR . . . . HELPS TAKE THE WEIGHT OFF YOUR WRISTS."

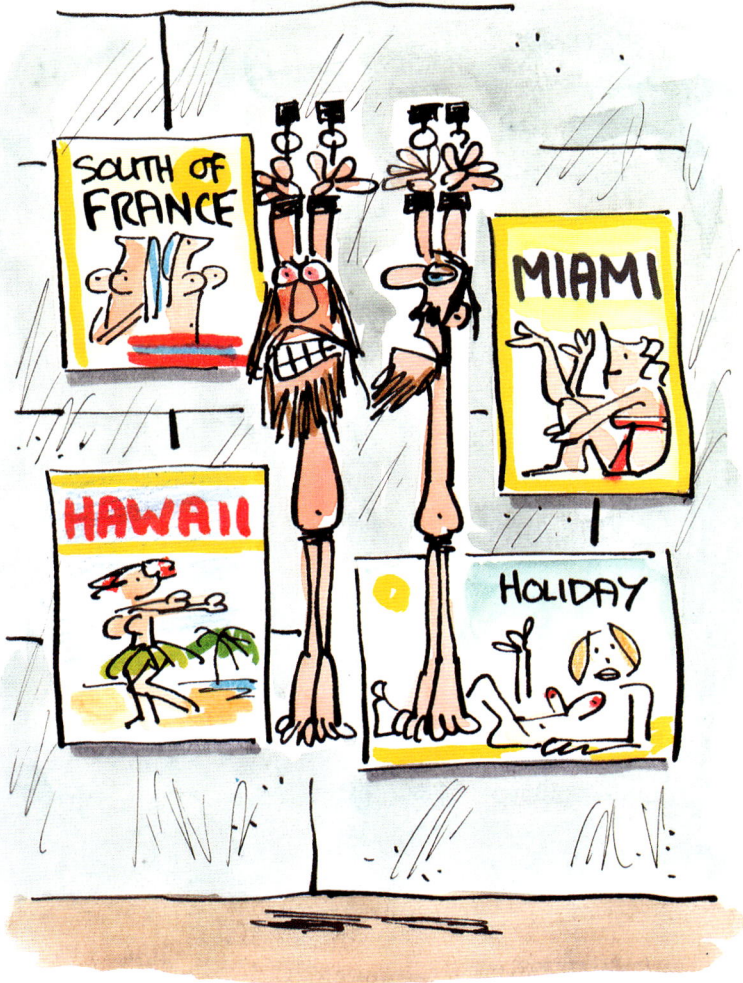

"OF ALL THE GUARDS IN THE PRISON SERVICE, WE HAVE TO END UP WITH THE SADISTIC BASTARD."

"DAMN! LOOKS LIKE WE'RE IN FOR
ANOTHER EPIDEMIC."

"I THOUGHT US KIDNEY DONOR CARD CARRIERS HAD TO BE DEAD FIRST?"

"I CAN STAND THE PHYSICAL TORTURE, BUT THIS PSYCHOLOGICAL STUFF IS KILLING ME!"

"STAY PERFECTLY STILL .... THEY CAN STRIP THE SKIN OFF ANYTHING THAT MOVES!"

"YOU'VE MASTERED THE SWING . . . NOW CONCENTRATE ON THE DROP."

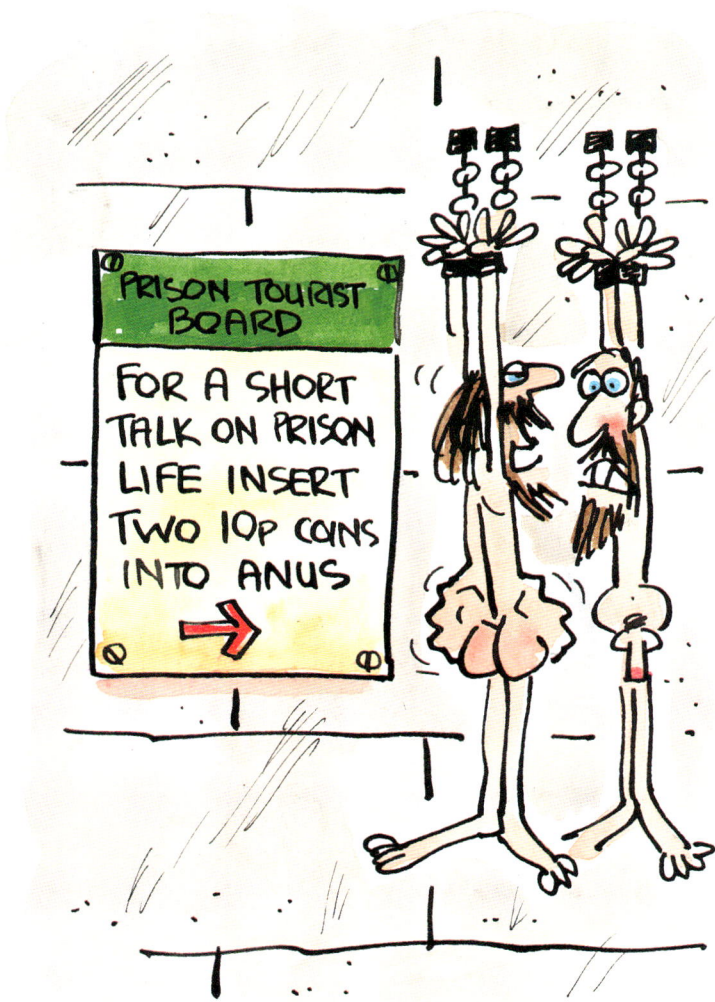

"IT'S A NICE LITTLE EARNER .... BUT I SUFFER A BIT FROM CONSTIPATION."

"YOU SHOULD NEVER HAVE ASKED 'EM FOR A DIRTY WEEKEND."

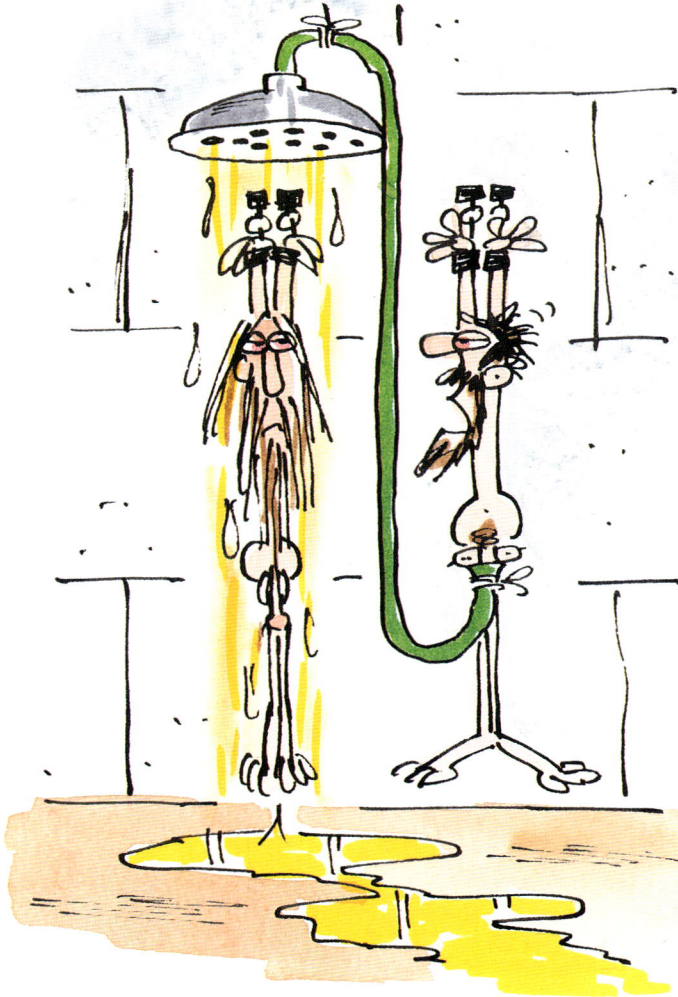

"THE SWINES ARE TRYING TO BREAK UP
OUR FRIENDSHIP."

"TAKE A TIP FROM ME, SON. NEVER GET INVOLVED WITH THE GOVERNOR'S WIFE."

"YES, BUT DOUBLE PUNISHMENT REALLY STARTS WHEN YOU PISS ....."

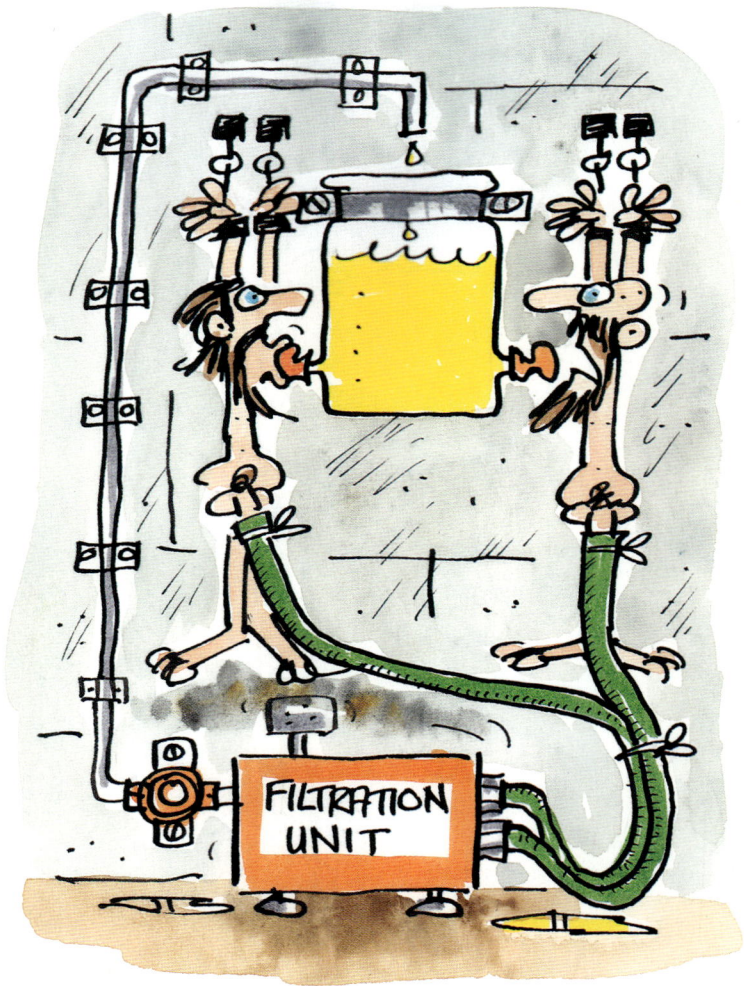

"THEY'RE TRYING IT WITH THE SOLID STUFF TOO . . . . BUT IT KEEPS CLOGGING UP!"

"SORRY ABOUT THAT . . . . I'M AN EX-BARMAN, SO I EXPECTED YOU TO SAY 'WHEN'."

"IT MUST BE SUMMER .... I'M GETTING A
BIT OF A SUN TAN."

"RIGHT, I'M OFF ON SIX WEEKS HOLIDAY THEN .... EAT VERY VERY SLOWLY AND YOU'LL BE JUST FINE."

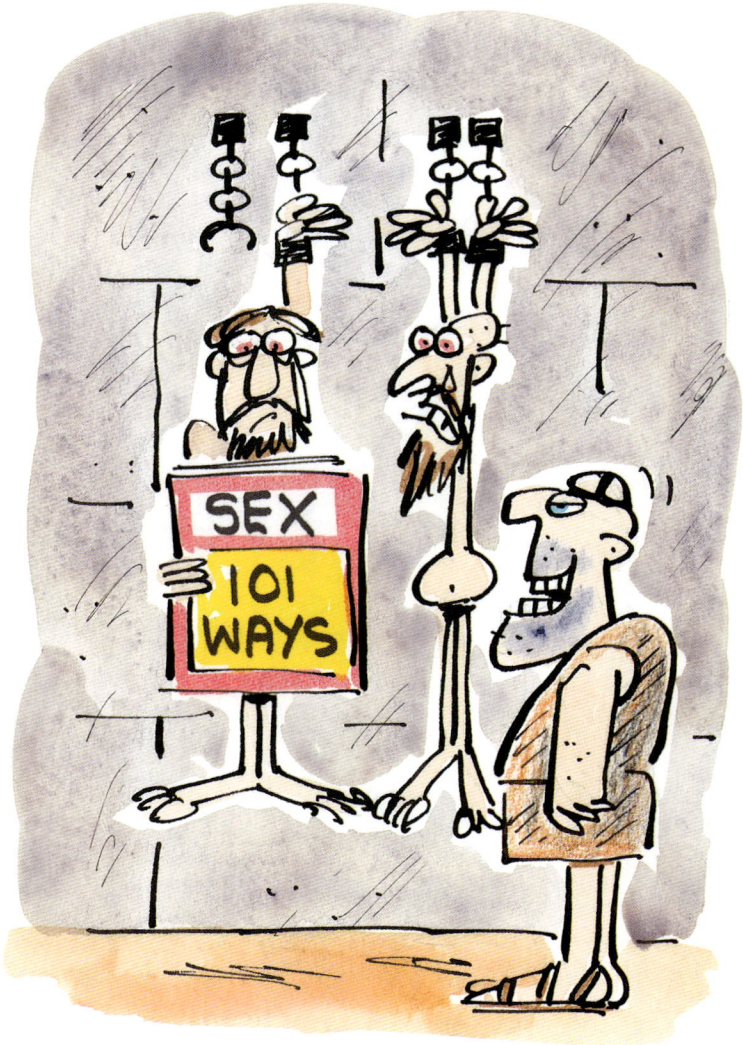

"LIKE IT? THE LIBRARIAN SAID YOU LIKED READING TEAR-JERKERS."

"THE THING YOU'LL MISS MOST IS A NORMAL SEX LIFE."

"THEY CERTAINLY KNOW HOW TO MAKE A CHAP FEEL MISERABLE."

"PRAT! I TOLD YOU NOT TO KICK UP A FUSS FOR A BLOW DRYER!"

"THIS SUBSIDENCE MAY NOT WORRY YOU,
BROTHER . . . . BUT IT SCARES THE SHIT
OUT OF ME!"

"THE TAX PEOPLE HAVE YOU LISTED AS A WHOLESALER."

"THIS NEW FEMALE GOVERNOR MAKES ME SICK!"

"YES, I'VE STILL GOT APPENDICITIS . . . THE SURGEONS PERMANENTLY PISSED ON THE JOB!"

"HOW DO YOU LIKE SOLITARY THEN?"

"I PUT YOUR NAME DOWN FOR A SEX-CHANG OP . . . . I LIKE FEMALE COMPANY."

"YES, IT IS LIKE WATCHING TV . . . . . ALL
REPEATS! WINTER, SPRING, SUMMER,
AUTUMN, WINTER, SPRING . . . . . "

"I'VE SERVED MY TIME, BUT THE BITCH WON'T LET ME GO."

"ONE DAY, SON . . . . ALL THIS WILL BE YOURS."

"IT'S THE GOVERNORS IDEA . . . HE WANTS YOU TO LOOK HAPPY!"

"I SUPPOSE THEY HAVE TO TREAT THE ARISTOCRACY A BIT DIFFERENT TO US LOT!"

"HE'S OUT ON PAROLE."

"LOOKS LIKE THEY DON'T EXPECT YOU TO KEEP YOUR NOSE CLEAN."

OTHER TITLES AVAILABLE FROM IDEAS UNLIMITED (PUBLISHING)

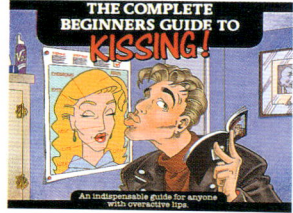

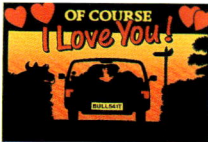

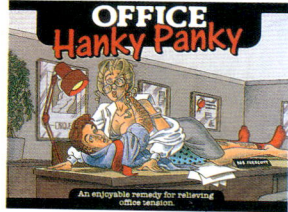

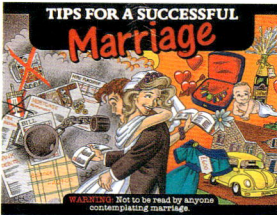

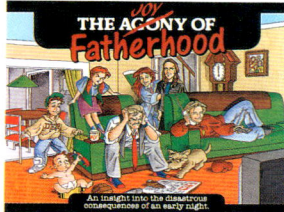

Please send me:

☐ copy/copies of **"WELL HUNG"** ISBN 1–871964–07–5 (96 pages A5) Full Colour   @ **£2.99** (postage free)

☐ copy/copies of **"THE BODY LANGUAGE SEX SIGNALS"** ISBN 1 – 871964–06–7   @ **£2.50** (postage free)

☐ copy/copies of **"100 Chat Up Lines"** ISBN 1–871964–00–8 (128 pages A7)   @ **£1.99** (postage free)

☐ copy/copies of **"Of course I Love You"** ISBN 1–871964–01–6 (96 pages A6)   @ **£1.99** (postage free)

☐ copy/copies of **"The Beginners Guide to Kissing"** ISBN 1–871964–02–4 (64 pages A5)   @ **£2.50** (postage free)

☐ copy/copies of **"Tips for a Successful Marriage"** ISBN 1–871964–03–2 (64 pages A5)   @ **£2.50** (postage free)

☐ copy/copies of **"The Joy of Fatherhood"** ISBN 1–871964–04–0 (64 pages A5)   @ **£2.50** (postage free)

☐ copy/copies of **"Office Hanky Panky"** ISBN 1–871964–05–9 (64 pages A5)   @ **£2.50** (postage free)

I Have enclosed a cheque/postal order for **£** . . . . made payable to Ideas Unlimited (Publishing)

Name: . . . .

Address: . . . .

Fill in the coupon and send it with your payment to: **Ideas Unlimited (Publishing) PO Box 125, Portsmouth POI 4PP**

**LOOK OUT FOR
THE
WELL HUNG
SERIES OF
GREETING CARDS.**

OTHER TITLES AVAILABLE FROM IDEAS UNLIMITED (PUBLISHING)

WELL HUNG

CHAIN GANG   Cartoons by FERRELLS

100 CHAT UP Lines

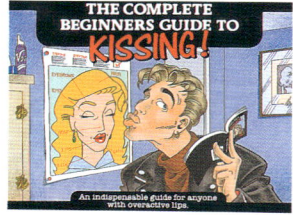

THE COMPLETE BEGINNERS GUIDE TO KISSING!

An indispensable guide for anyone with overactive lips.

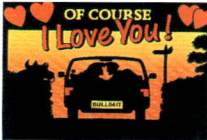

OF COURSE I Love You!

BODY LANGUAGE SEX Signals for the brash

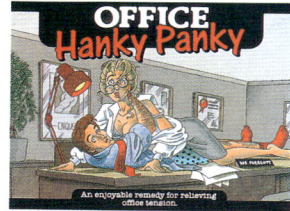

OFFICE Hanky Panky

An enjoyable remedy for relieving office tension.

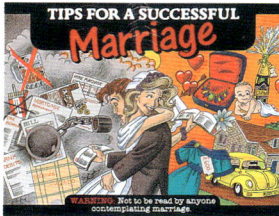

TIPS FOR A SUCCESSFUL Marriage

WARNING: Not to be read by anyone contemplating marriage.

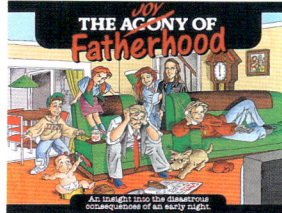

THE Joy AGONY OF Fatherhood

An insight into the disastrous consequences of an early night.

Please send me:

☐ copy/copies of **"WELL HUNG"** ISBN 1–871964–07–5 (96 pages A5) Full Colour — @ **£2.99** (postage free)
☐ copy/copies of **"THE BODY LANGUAGE SEX SIGNALS"** ISBN 1 – 871964–06–7 — @ **£2.50** (postage free)
☐ copy/copies of **"100 Chat Up Lines"** ISBN 1–871964–00–8 (128 pages A7) — @ **£1.99** (postage free)
☐ copy/copies of **"Of course I Love You"** ISBN 1–871964–01–6 (96 pages A6) — @ **£1.99** (postage free)
☐ copy/copies of **"The Beginners Guide to Kissing"** ISBN 1–871964–02–4 (64 pages A5) — @ **£2.50** (postage free)
☐ copy/copies of **"Tips for a Successful Marriage"** ISBN 1–871964–03–2 (64 pages A5) — @ **£2.50** (postage free)
☐ copy/copies of **"The Joy of Fatherhood"** ISBN 1–871964–04–0 (64 pages A5) — @ **£2.50** (postage free)
☐ copy/copies of **"Office Hanky Panky"** ISBN 1–871964–05–9 (64 pages A5) — @ **£2.50** (postage free)

I Have enclosed a cheque/postal order for **£** . . . . made payable to Ideas Unlimited (Publishing)

Name: . . . .

Address: . . . .

Fill in the coupon and send it with your payment to: **Ideas Unlimited (Publishing) PO Box 125, Portsmouth PO1 4PP**

**LOOK OUT FOR
THE
WELL HUNG
SERIES OF
GREETING CARDS.**